# zenda

## and the Gazing Ball

Dedicated to:
# Rose & Mickey
# Johnny & Gena

Thank you to:
Birdie for divine intervention.
Broadthink for professional guidance.
Charlotte Kalnit & Caspar Ouvaroff for
behind-the-scenes magic at Amodeo Petti.
Pam Amodeo. Mary Ann Wheaton & Blue Digital for
supernatural covers. Nina & Nessa, Molly & Gigi,
Jesse & Gabriel, Paige Sophia & Kaitlin Eliott &
Danny, Dylan & Ashley for inspiration.

# zenda

### and the Gazing Ball

*created by*
*Ken Petti and John Amodeo*

*written with*
*Cassandra Westwood*

Grosset & Dunlap • New York

Copyright © 2004 by Ken Petti & John Amodeo. All rights reserved. Published by Grosset & Dunlap, a division of Penguin Young Readers Group, 345 Hudson Street, New York, New York 10014. GROSSET & DUNLAP is a trademark of Penguin Group (USA) Inc. Printed in the U.S.A.

Library of Congress Cataloging-in-Publication Data

Petti, Ken.
  Zenda and the gazing ball / created by Ken Petti and John Amodeo ; written with Cassandra Westwood.
      p. cm. — (Zenda ; 1)
Summary: Twelve-year-old Zenda of Azureblue, a magical planet, looks forward to her gazing ball ceremony to reveal the unique lessons to guide her through life, but when she breaks her gazing ball, the future seems lost.
  ISBN 0-448-43223-4 (pbk.)
  [1. Fantasy.]  I. Amodeo, John, 1949 May 19– II. Westwood, Cassandra. III. Title.
  PZ7.P448125Ze 2004
  [Fic]—dc22

                            2003015048

      ISBN 0-448-43223-4                    A B C D E F G H I J

# Contents

Since the day I turned twelve, I've only been able to think of one thing: my gazing ball ceremony. It's the most important day in the life of anybody growing up here on Azureblue.

I couldn't wait to get my gazing ball. Each ball reveals thirteen musings—they're like little bits of advice that will help you on your life's journey. When all thirteen musings are learned, the gazing ball reveals something incredible: your special, hidden gift. Every person on Azureblue is born with a special power. The gazing ball holds the key to that power.

I was really anxious to get my gazing ball and find out what secrets it held for me. But I guess I got too anxious and, well . . . what was supposed to be the best day of my life turned out to be the worst day ever.

So here's the story of what happened. I think things kind of worked out in the end, but . . . you can see for yourself.

Cosmically yours,
Zenda

———∞∞∞———

_Impatience_

*Zenda sailed above the white clouds, riding on the back of a giant bird the color of an amethyst. Her red hair streamed behind her, gleaming against the brilliant blue sky. The green trees and gardens of the village looked like patchwork pieces on the ground. She waved to the people below, waved and waved as the bird took her away to mysterious new places . . .*

"Zenda! Didn't you hear Marion Rose? It's time for our first gazing ball class."

The words "gazing ball" snapped Zenda out of her daydream. She looked up from her table to see Camille, her best friend, looking at her with worried brown eyes.

"Everyone's outside," Camille said. "Come on!"

Camille grabbed Zenda's arm and practically pulled her out of her chair. The girls ran through the learning building out into the bright sunlight.

The Cobalt School for Girls looked like most other schools on the planet Azureblue, with four U-shaped buildings forming a circle around a very wide and very tall willow tree. The girls in Zenda's class were seated on the soft grass beneath the tree's cascading branches. Every girl wore a crown of colorful flowers on her head. The girls' teacher, Marion Rose, sat on a smooth, gray rock. She held a small wooden box in her hands.

"Zenda, you're late!" The teacher's words were stern, but her voice was warm. "I thought you of all people would be anxious to have your first gazing ball lesson."

Some of the girls laughed good-naturedly, and Zenda blushed. All the girls had been excited about the gazing ball ceremony for weeks now, but Zenda seemed to think and talk about it more than anyone else. Marion Rose had caught Zenda daydreaming about the ceremony many times before.

"Sorry, Marion Rose," Zenda said. She and Camille found an empty patch of grass and sat down.

"As I was saying," the teacher continued,

"every child on Azureblue receives a gazing ball the day he or she is born. The balls are kept under lock and key until that child turns twelve-and-a-half. Then there is a . . ."

"Gazing ball ceremony!" some of the girls cried out. Zenda smiled. She wasn't the only one excited about the ceremony.

"That's right," Marion Rose said, smiling, too. With her round face, sparkling blue eyes, and blonde hair that she wore in a long braid down her back, Zenda often thought her teacher looked more like a student.

Marion Rose opened the wooden box. She took out a glass sphere the size of an apple. The gazing ball glittered in the sunlight.

"This is a sample gazing ball," Marion said. "I'll pass it around. Your gazing balls will look similar, but each person's gazing ball is unique."

One of the girls raised her hand. "Can't we see our own gazing balls now?"

The teacher shook her head. "Not until

the night of the gazing ball ceremony. It's . . . unwise to handle your gazing ball without proper guidance. That's why we're using the sample ball today."

The girls carefully passed the ball from one to another. When Zenda got the ball, she held it up to catch the light.

Inside the ball, she could see a tiny reflection of herself. A crown of bluebells rested in the waves of her reddish-gold hair. She had chosen the flowers—and her dress— to match the blue in her eyes.

For a second, Zenda felt like the reflection inside the ball was staring back at her—another Zenda with a life all her own. The feeling gave her goose bumps. She quickly passed the gazing ball to Camille.

"Two days from now, you will be given your gazing balls in a special ceremony," Marion Rose said. "It's traditional for friends and family to be present when the gazing balls are presented to you. It's also traditional to celebrate with a party afterwards."

A murmur of excitement rose up among the girls.

Marion Rose continued. "For the next six months, you will carry your gazing ball with you at all times. Your ball will reveal thirteen musings—thirteen secrets about who you are and who you're destined to become. Can anyone tell me more about the musings?"

"I can!" came a voice from behind Zenda. She didn't need to turn around to know who it was. Alexandra White's mother was headmistress of the Cobalt School for Girls. As a result, Alex acted like she knew everything about everything.

"The musings are special messages that relate to our lives," Alexandra said. She sounded like she was reciting from a book.

"Right, Alex," said Marion Rose. "Your musings will be revealed one at a time. Once you receive a musing, you will study it to learn its meaning. And once all thirteen musings are learned, on your thirteenth birthday the gazing ball will reveal . . .

"Our special gift." Zenda found herself saying the words in time with the teacher, and she blushed again.

The special gift was the reason Zenda was so excited about the gazing ball ceremony. Everyone on Azureblue had a gift, and the kind of gift you had determined your path in life.

Marion Rose nodded in Zenda's direction. "Actually, Zenda, you have some experience with your gift already, don't you? Would you like to share that with us?"

Zenda felt like sinking into the ground. About two years ago, she had started to show signs of *kani*—a special ability to communicate with plants. It was almost unheard of for anyone to show signs of their gift before their thirteenth birthday.

Zenda's parents had been thrilled, of course. But Zenda had mixed feelings about it. For one thing, she wasn't exactly an expert at *kani* yet, and things went wrong all the time. For another, if *kani* was her gift, that meant she would spend her life growing and caring for plants, and well . . . she wasn't sure she wanted that.

"It's not such a big deal," Zenda replied shyly. "I can do things with plants—help them grow. Or change the way they look. But it doesn't always work."

"Well, I think it's wonderful," Marion Rose said, beaming.

"Sounds more like a freak to me," Alexandra whispered in a voice just loud enough for Zenda to hear.

Zenda felt her face flush.

Suddenly, the girls in the circle burst out laughing.

Zenda looked around, bewildered.

"It's your flower crown," Camille whispered.

Zenda plucked a flower off her crown. Instead of a tiny bluebell flower, she held a bright red poppy blossom in her hand. Zenda guessed the flower was as red as her face felt.

It was a side effect of her gift. Her mood could actually change the plants around her — and usually did at the worst times.

Marion Rose gave Zenda a sympathetic smile. "Every gift needs time to mature," she said. "I think it's rather lovely, actually."

"Thanks," Zenda muttered, but she was sure the teacher was just trying to make her feel better.

To Zenda's relief, nothing else embarrassing happened in class. Marion Rose talked more about the gazing ball ceremony and answered questions until, finally, school let out for the day.

Zenda and Camille walked home along a tree-lined path. The soothing waters of Crystal Creek bubbled alongside the path.

"Don't listen to Alexandra, Zen," Camille said as they walked. "She's just jealous."

It was hard for Zenda to imagine tall,

popular Alex being jealous of anyone. Alexandra was perfect in just about every way. Her hair was never knotty or tangled. Her dresses were never wrinkled. She got excellent grades in every class. She had lots of friends. Why Alex needed to make mean comments all the time absolutely puzzled Zenda. That most of Alex's comments were directed toward Zenda puzzled her even more.

"I don't know," Zenda replied. "Maybe she's right. Maybe I am a freak!"

"Don't say that!" Camille cried. "You are not a freak. I think your gift is amazing."

"Thanks," Zenda said, smiling gratefully. Camille always made her feel better.

"Can you come over today?" Camille asked. "Mom and I are designing a new dress for the ceremony. You can come help us if you want."

Zenda shook her head. Going to Camille's house was always fun, but there was something she wanted to do.

"No, thanks," she replied. "But I can't wait

to see it!" Camille's mother was a dressmaker who owned a small shop in the village. Zenda thought she made the prettiest dresses on Azureblue.

"Okay," Camille called out as she disappeared around a bend. "Just forget all about what Alex said!"

But Zenda couldn't forget. She took off her crown and tossed it into the creek, watching the water carry the red flowers away. Then she took a branch with tightly closed apple blossom buds from a nearby tree, formed it into a circle, and put the new crown on her head.

Zenda sat down at the base of the tree and took a small book out of her schoolbag. A gift from her mother, the journal was covered in purple silk—Zenda's favorite color—and her name was stamped on it in gold. Zenda untied the cream-colored ribbons that kept the journal closed, opened the book, and began to write.

Now, more than ever, I can't wait until the gazing ball ceremony. I keep wondering what my special gift will be. Will it be kani?

I know that's what everyone expects. They think I'll spend my life working with plants. But I can't help it if I want more. When I was born, my mother said there were tiny stars twinkling in my eyes. They faded after a few days, but I don't think they ever really left me. I wonder if that's why I can't seem to keep my feet on the ground.

I want a gift that will carry me away, like the bird in my dreams . . .

*Two days is too long to wait for the ceremony! The sooner I get my gazing ball, the sooner this whole journey will begin.*

*I want to find out now!!!*

As Zenda punctuated the journal page with exclamation points, she heard a popping sound above her head. She lifted off the apple blossom crown to see that her feelings of impatience had caused all of the tiny closed buds to burst open.

Zenda sighed. "Not again!"

*Expectations*

Zenda closed her journal and headed back on the path toward home. The sweet smell of the freshly opened apple blossoms tickled her nose.

Soon a faded log fence came into view. The fence bordered a huge field, lush with the green plants and colorful flowers that Zenda's parents grew for their business. Azureblue Karmaceuticals was the most successful company of its kind in the universe. It seemed to Zenda that her parents, Verbena and Vetiver, spent every spare moment creating new formulas for healing tonics or developing new scents for their aromatherapy line.

Beyond the field was a cluster of buildings that formed the heart of the company: two glass greenhouses; a long, low building where the formulas were made; a cheerful, red barn where the products were packaged; and a row of small, stone cottages inhabited by the company's employees.

Overlooking it all, atop a small hill, sat Zenda's home: a tall, wooden house with a round cupola rising from the second floor. Zenda's mother, Verbena, had painted the house in several different shades of green, her favorite color.

As Zenda approached, she saw Verbena waving to her in front of the barn. Zenda ran up and kissed her mother on the cheek. Verbena wore her usual working outfit—a plain, short-sleeved top and a long skirt that reached her ankles—today, it was yellow. Her long, brown hair hung down to her waist.

"Mykal's having trouble with the red rosebushes in the garden," Verbena said. "Why don't you see if you can help him?"

"Sure," Zenda said, trying to sound casual.

So Mykal was here. Zenda shouldn't have been surprised. Mykal was her neighbor and friend, and attended the Cobalt School for Boys right next to the girls' school. Since Mykal's parents died a year ago, Mykal spent most of his spare time helping Zenda's parents in the garden. Mykal loved plants almost as much as her parents did—maybe more. No matter what his gift turned out to be, he intended to somehow involve plants in his future. That's why he spent most days after school working with Verbena and Vetiver at Azureblue Karmaceuticals. Mykal liked to learn about fertilizers and soil types and weather patterns—all of the things that made Zenda start daydreaming.

Zenda's stomach fluttered every time she saw Mykal, although she wasn't exactly sure why. He was nice, and funny and cute, too— but he always seemed to be thinking about something else when Zenda was around. She wondered if it was because he was so obsessed with plants.

Zenda found Mykal leaning over a scraggly-looking rosebush, pouring a thick, green liquid onto its roots. His shaggy, sandy-blond hair hung over his eyes. He didn't notice Zenda until she tapped him on his shoulder.

"Hey!" Mykal said, turning around.

"Sorry, I didn't see you. I was just trying out a new growth formula. I upped the nutrient content. These babies really need help."

"It looks like you've got it under control," Zenda said. But inside she was thinking, *How can his eyes possibly be so green? They look like emeralds.*

Mykal shook his head. "I don't know. I thought maybe you could try using your gift."

Zenda nervously bit her bottom lip. "It doesn't always work, you know," she said.

"Please try," Mykal said. "It can't hurt. I saw what you did with those peach trees last year."

Zenda took a deep breath. She could at least try.

"Okay," she said. She closed her eyes and placed her hands on the rosebush. She was never exactly sure how she knew what to do. She just kind of followed her feelings.

Zenda started to get a feeling from the plant—a feeling like hunger.

*Mykal was right,* Zenda realized.

*These bushes do need more nutrients.*

Zenda imagined the nutrients coursing through the stems of the rosebush, pouring into the leaves and flowers. She imagined new leaves and flowers sprouting on the stems. Her hands grew warm as she concentrated her thoughts.

"It's working!" Mykal exclaimed.

Zenda opened her eyes. Some of the branches had started to snake outward, growing new leaves. Fat rosebuds on the end of the stems were starting to open.

"It's so easy for you," Mykal murmured, and Zenda thought she detected a hint of frustration in his voice.

Then the rosebuds opened—into bright, blue flowers!

Zenda groaned. "Oh, no. I'm so sorry!"

"That's weird," Mykal said, closely examining one of the flowers. "The plant is definitely healthier. But why would the color change?"

"I told you it didn't always work," Zenda said, backing away from the bush. "Listen, I'd better get out of here before I start turning bluebells orange or something."

Absorbed by the rosebush, Mykal didn't even seem to notice as Zenda left the garden.

"He must think I'm hopeless," Zenda muttered as she headed toward the house. She could sense the apple blossoms on her head beginning to wilt.

Then a welcome sight made her smile. A small brown dog bounded off the front porch, barking and wagging his tail.

"Hi, Oscar," Zenda said. "Did you miss me today?"

Oscar trotted at Zenda's heels as she walked inside the house. She found her father, Vetiver, chopping vegetables in the kitchen.

"Feel like peeling some carrots, starshine?" he asked, calling Zenda by her childhood nickname.

"Sure, Dad," Zenda replied. She knew she

could prep carrots without messing up, at least.

About an hour later, Zenda sat with her parents in the screened-in dining room, eating a plate of pasta and vegetables doused with Vetiver's famous herb cream sauce, Zenda's favorite. Oscar sat at Zenda's feet, waiting to catch the scraps she would sneak him.

"I can't believe your gazing ball ceremony is only two nights away!" Verbena said, smiling.

Zenda nodded excitedly. "I can't wait! It seems like it will never happen."

"It'll be here before you know it," Verbena assured her. A dreamy look crossed her face. "If you ask me, it's come much too quickly. It seems like only yesterday you were a baby in my arms."

Zenda grimaced and took a bite of carrot. Why did mothers always want to talk about when you were a baby? She was almost thirteen!

"It's coming too fast for me, too," Vetiver

said. "I've still got so much cooking to do before the big party. Those avocado sandwiches won't make themselves."

Zenda wrinkled her nose. "Avocado sandwiches?"

"They're Mykal's favorite," Vetiver said. "It's his party, too, you know."

After Mykal's parents died, he had moved in with his Great Aunt Tess. Verbena and Vetiver had offered to hold a party for both Zenda and Mykal to make things easier for Tess.

"That reminds me," said Verbena. "How did things go out in the rose garden today?"

Zenda slurped down her last piece of pasta.

"Um . . . good and bad," she answered.

Vetiver smiled. "Tell us the good first," he said.

"The roses got bigger," Zenda said.

"And the bad?" Verbena asked.

Zenda avoided their eyes. "Well, the flowers came out kind of . . . blue."

Her parents laughed. Vetiver patted her

on the shoulder.

"Don't worry," he said. "I'm sure you'll get the hang of your gift soon. Why, I bet you'll be a *kani* expert after you complete your gazing ball training."

"You know, I might get a completely different gift after my gazing ball training," Zenda said, feeling defensive. "We don't know for sure."

"Of course," Verbena said gently. "But, Zenda, you do have signs of *kani*. And it's such a rare and beautiful gift—the most treasured gift on the planet. You'd be lucky to get it."

"All life on Azureblue depends on plants," Vetiver said. Zenda had heard this lecture many times before. "Our food. Our clothes. And, of course, our medicines. We have almost no disease on Azureblue, and that is directly due to our ability to extract the healing powers of plants. Without healthy plants, our planet—even our universe—would be in serious trouble."

Zenda sighed. Of course she loved plants. She knew what her parents did made a difference in the world.

But what was so wrong about wanting more?

# Temptation

The next morning, Zenda rose with the sun. Normally, it took Oscar licking her face to get her out of bed, but not today. Today was officially one day away from the gazing ball ceremony. Zenda figured the sooner she woke up, the sooner the day of the ceremony would come.

Zenda took a bath, towel-dried her hair, and slipped on a sleeveless, light yellow dress. In the garden alongside the house, she picked seven daisies to make into a crown.

"Please don't change on me today," Zenda instructed the daisies as she wove their stems together. Her changing flower crowns were a constant source of embarrassment, yet it would have been worse not to wear one at all. Every girl her age on the planet wore a flower crown. Zenda would have felt bald without one.

After a breakfast of azureberry pancakes, Zenda patted Oscar good-bye, waved to her parents, and headed down the path. She looked for Mykal, who often walked to school with her, but he was nowhere in sight.

"He probably thinks I'm a freak, too," Zenda sighed, then immediately shook off the mood. Today was a beautiful day, and soon she would have her gazing ball.

Zenda continued down the path and walked to the Commons, a circle-shaped park in the middle of their village. Zenda had always thought that the pathways in her village were laid out like a spiderweb. They all started from the Commons Circle and branched out in all directions, crisscrossing each other. But each path led back to the center.

As Zenda walked, she could see the leaves of the trees rustle as the trees responded to her excitement. Up ahead, a patch of wild chicory flowers turned their bluish-purple heads toward her, as though they were saying hello.

Zenda couldn't help smiling. She had to admit that her gift, however strange, was a pretty wonderful thing sometimes.

Soon the Cobalt School for Girls came into view. Camille stood under the willow tree, waiting for Zenda.

Zenda smiled and ran toward her friend. Camille wore a nut-brown dress a shade darker than her skin. Her thick black curls were accented with a circle of colorful flowers.

But as Zenda got closer, she saw that they weren't just flowers. Five butterflies, each a different color, were perched on top of Camille's flower crown. Camille had her eyes closed and was softly murmuring something Zenda couldn't quite make out.

"Wow," Zenda said softly. "That's beautiful, Cam."

Camille smiled and opened her eyes. "It's for my project," she explained. Once kids on Azureblue turned twelve, they began a program of independent study. Each student picked one topic, such as the waters of Azureblue or the history of Azureblue's people, and explored it through the disciplines of math, science, and language, plus any other special talents they had. Camille had chosen ethno-entomology—the study of the insect world. She loved flying, crawling creatures as much as Mykal loved plants. More than anything, Camille wanted to be able to communicate with insects the way that Zenda could communicate with plants.

"You're doing great," Zenda said, spellbound as the butterflies gently moved their wings.

"I started out by sketching them," Camille explained. Zenda knew her friend was a talented artist. "But then Marion Rose taught me a trick for communicating with them. It just takes concentration. I can't believe it works!"

All at once, the butterflies lifted off and fluttered away.

"I can't believe you can concentrate on anything," Zenda said. "All I can think about is the gazing ball ceremony."

Camille shook her head. "I'm trying not to think about it. I'm so nervous!" she replied. "We're going to have to stand up in front of everybody at the ceremony tomorrow. What if I trip and fall? Or what if I take the wrong ball? Or what if—"

"You're going to be fine," Zenda said, patting her shoulder. "Come on, let's go in."

The girls walked into the Sage Building, marked with a picture of a leafy sage plant on the door. Inside, sunlight streamed through rows of tall windows, illuminating long, L-shaped desks covered with books, papers, flowers, rocks, and anything else the girls were studying. The learning stations were open and inviting, designed to encourage students to work together. Teachers on Azureblue firmly believed that sharing ideas was the key to learning.

Zenda's classmates wandered around the learning stations, waiting for Marion Rose to begin the day. Each girl wore a flower crown on her head, but otherwise, each girl was unique. Some, like Alexandra White, were as tall and slender as sunflowers; some were small and delicate, like lilies of the valley. All of the girls wore a variety of colorful clothing, from long, flowing skirts to paint-splattered overalls to the simple dresses that Zenda and Camille preferred.

Marion Rose entered. Pencils, paint-brushes, and flowers sprouted from her long blonde braid, as though she had stuck them there and forgot about them. She wore a white shirt covered by a jumper that she had dyed with a rainbow of plant hues.

"Good morning, girls," the teacher said, smiling. "Get on your mats, please. I think we need some grounding today."

Zenda and Camille hurried to the learning stations. Zenda pulled out a mat of soft, woven reeds and set it on the floor. She and the other girls sat on their mats, cross-legged.

"I want you to close your eyes," Marion Rose said. "Now imagine that there are roots growing out of your legs. The roots are sinking deep into the ground, into the dark brown earth . . ."

Zenda tried to picture the roots in her mind, but it wasn't easy. The grounding exercise was supposed to help students focus for the rest of the day, but Marion Rose's soothing voice had the effect of luring Zenda to sleep. She was about to drift off when the teacher announced that the exercise was over. Zenda yawned, stretched, and stood up.

"I want everyone to focus this morning," Marion Rose instructed. "I know tomorrow is a big day, but we still have things to accomplish today. Please begin work on your independent study projects until it's time for herbology class."

Zenda turned to her learning station and pulled out the diagram of the solar system she had begun to map. Zenda had chosen to study astronomy for her project—the stars and planets in the universe outside Azureblue. Thirteen planets, including Azureblue, revolved around the sun. Zenda had plotted the sun in the center of the diagram, and was using a compass to plot the circular orbits of the planets around it. She had developed a scale of measurement, a starting point for determining where to plot each orbit on the diagram.

Normally, math came easy to Zenda. There was something comforting about how predictable the numbers were; if you knew the right equations, you could figure out anything. Math made sense out of a complicated universe. But today, the numbers on her worksheet seemed to dance and swirl on the paper, escaping examination.

Zenda soon realized she wasn't the only one who couldn't focus. The sound of whispers echoed around the room, and Zenda knew all of the girls were talking about the same thing—their gazing balls.

Zenda walked across the room to Camille's learning station. Her friend was busily writing in a journal.

"How can you work?" Zenda asked her. "I can't stop thinking about tomorrow!"

Camille smiled sheepishly and pushed her journal toward Zenda. Camille had drawn a picture of herself holding her gazing ball in her palm.

Zenda giggled. "Okay. I guess I'm not alone."

"You want to find out about your gazing ball?" said a voice from behind Zenda.

Zenda turned to see Alexandra White standing there. It wasn't often that Alex started a conversation with Zenda. In fact, Alex was usually whispering things behind Zenda's back. Zenda inwardly winced as she remembered Alex's comment from yesterday.

"Of course I want to find out about my gazing ball," Zenda said cautiously. "Doesn't everybody?"

Alex nodded and stepped closer. Her bright, dark eyes seemed to bore through Zenda. Her long, chestnut brown hair gleamed in the morning sunlight.

"I know how we can see the gazing balls before tomorrow," Alex whispered. She pulled out a chain that was tucked under her dress. A silver key dangled from the chain.

"This key opens the door to the room where the gazing balls are kept," Alex continued. "Some of the girls and I are going to sneak in tonight. Are you in?" The question sounded like a dare.

"Are you kidding?" Camille asked. "We'll get in so much trouble. No thanks. Right, Zenda?"

Camille looked at Zenda for confirmation, but Zenda didn't reply right away.

She had no reason to trust Alex. Still, the idea intrigued her. If she went along with Alex, she could see her gazing ball. Tonight! No more waiting. But, still . . .

"Why are you asking us?" Zenda asked suspiciously.

Alex shrugged. "Why not?" she said. "I don't know about your friend here, but I thought you just might be daring enough to do it, Zenda."

Zenda wasn't expecting that reply. It sounded almost like a compliment.

But Camille was right. Whether Alex was sincere or not, it was still a bad idea.

"No, thanks," Zenda said finally. "I can wait until tomorrow like everyone else."

Alex shrugged.

"Your loss," she said, and walked away.

Marion Rose walked over to the learning station, shaking her head. "I hope you girls are sharing ideas, but something tells me you're not focusing," she said.

"Sorry, teacher," Zenda said quickly. She waved good-bye to Camille and walked back to her station.

Zenda reached for her diagram when

something caught her eye. There was a folded piece of paper on the table. Zenda scooped up the paper and opened it under the table. It read:

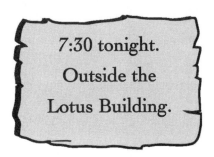

7:30 tonight.
Outside the
Lotus Building.

Zenda's heart beat a little faster. The note had to be from Alex.

Zenda crumpled up the note. Trusting Alex was just silly.

Still . . . Zenda smoothed out the note and tucked it into her pocket. After all, it was just a little peek at the gazing balls. That couldn't hurt.

Could it?

Later, as she walked home from school, Alex's offer tugged at Zenda's thoughts. *7:30 tonight.* In just a few hours, Zenda could see her gazing ball if she wanted to. It would be so simple . . .

Zenda sighed. She wished she had someone to talk to. She already knew how Camille felt about the plan. If only her grandmother was alive. Delphina was Vetiver's mother, and she was always the one person who seemed to know exactly what Zenda was thinking, and just what to say when Zenda had a problem.

But Delphina had died just before Zenda's tenth birthday. It seemed so long ago now. Zenda liked to close her eyes and picture her grandmother's face: her blue eyes, just like Zenda's; her soft, wrinkled face; her snow-white hair. It was becoming harder and harder to keep the picture in focus, although Zenda knew that the memories of her grandmother would never fade. And Zenda still had Luna, the doll her grandmother had passed down to her.

*Of course, Luna,* Zenda realized. *I can tell Luna what's happened.*

When Zenda reached home, she went straight to her bedroom. Oscar followed behind as she climbed the stairs to her room.

Zenda had lived in this very room since she was a baby and she had always loved it, mostly because it adjoined the cupola. Zenda had made the small, round room her own, filling it with silk pillows the color of the sky and sea. Her favorite books rose from the floor in uneven stacks. Sheer pink and purple fabric was draped across the large windows.

Zenda's main bedroom contained her big, soft bed, which was covered with a canopy of living flowers. Lotions and potions from her parents' karmaceutical company covered the top of her large pine dresser. Zenda especially loved the pretty glass bottles of body elixirs, and she had one in every scent. The fact that her parents had insisted on putting Zenda's face on the label mostly pleased her, but sometimes made her embarrassed—especially when Alexandra White teased her about it.

Thinking of Alexandra reminded Zenda of why she had rushed to her room in the first place. She tossed her schoolbag on the floor next to her green velvet chair, where Oscar had curled up for a nap. Then she flopped down on the bed.

There, propped up against the pillows, was Luna.

Luna had been Delphina's doll when she was a baby. When Zenda was born, Delphina had given the doll to her. The little doll was made of scraps of colorful silk and stuffed with cotton mixed with herbs that had lost most of their scent long ago. Luna's round face wore a stitched-on smile that never wavered.

Zenda picked up Luna and looked into her green eyes. Since her grandmother had died, Zenda turned to Luna when she needed someone to talk to. Of course, Luna never answered back. But, somehow, talking with Luna helped Zenda feel connected to her grandmother—almost as though Delphina was alive again.

Zenda had never been able to explain it. Secretly, she wondered if a tiny bit of Delphina's spirit lived on in the doll.

"So what do you think, Luna?" Zenda asked. "Do you think I should take a peek at my gazing ball tonight?"

Luna stared back at Zenda, and Zenda closed her eyes. A peaceful, calm feeling immediately came over her body. A pink mist formed in her mind's eye. Through the mist, she could see Delphina, surrounded by white light.

*Don't be afraid to take chances, Zenda,* her adventurous grandmother had said more than once. *But always make sure those chances are worth taking.*

Zenda's eyes fluttered open. The Delphina she knew had never been afraid of anything.

She lived her life bravely and courageously.

But Delphina hadn't always been that way. Her grandmother had told her that she had been a cautious, timid child. Then she got her gazing ball, and the musings had helped her to blossom and change. In fact, Delphina's first musing—*don't be afraid to take chances*—had taught her to let go of her fears.

"Once I opened myself up to the world, I was able to accomplish anything I set my mind to," Delphina had said.

After Delphina learned her thirteen musings, her special gift had blossomed. Her grandmother was an artist who could convey all kinds of emotions through the colors in her paintings. Looking at one of Delphina's paintings could make you laugh, or feel peaceful, or even sad.

"The musings taught me to see the world in a whole new way," she had explained.

Of course, Delphina's musings had taught her to make wise choices, too.

"Every choice you make has consequences," she liked to tell Zenda. "I learned that lesson right after my first musing. Remember, Zenda, to think carefully before you act!"

And that advice was true of her grandmother as well. Delphina had traveled to all of the planets in the solar system, but she always returned home, safe and sound.

*Well*, Zenda reasoned, *I am thinking about it a lot, aren't I? And how could there possibly be any bad consequences?* It was just one little peek. It's not like she was going to do something terrible.

Zenda put Luna back on the pillows. Her mind was made up. She'd meet Alex at the Lotus Building at seven-thirty, take a quick look, and be home before eight.

And so, after dinner was finished and Zenda had dried the dishes, she told her parents she was going to Camille's to prepare for the gazing ball ceremony.

"Just for an hour," her mother had said. "You need to be well-rested for tomorrow."

Zenda had felt a twinge of guilt about lying to Verbena and Vetiver, but she brushed it aside. She wasn't a little girl anymore. It was time she started making her own decisions.

The sun's last rays were disappearing as Zenda headed down the path toward school. The sky overhead was a beautiful, deep blue. Ciro, the largest of Azureblue's four moons, was rising over the horizon.

Zenda knew that Ciro's soft glow would probably be enough to light the way, but to be safe she wandered off the path and found some moonglow vines snaking up a crumbling stone wall. The phosphorescent flowers of the plant gave off nearly as much light as one of the solar-powered lanterns her parents used at home. Zenda plucked one of the blooms. Its glow would last at least an hour, more if she put it in water.

Soon Zenda reached the school. In the

dark, the willow looked more like some giant, long-armed creature than a tree.

Zenda shuddered at the thought and made her way to the Lotus Building. The grounds seemed deserted, but as Zenda got closer she could make out three girls by the door.

"Zenda's here!" whispered one girl.

"Alex was right," whispered the other.

It was Gena and Astrid. The two girls couldn't have looked more like opposites. Gena was tall, dark, and athletic, while Astrid was short and pale with white-blonde hair. But they acted just like twins. The girls went everywhere and did everything together—and that usually meant following Alex around like lost puppies.

"You're just in time," Alex said, holding up the key. It glinted in the moonlight. "We're going in."

Zenda's heart quickened as Alex put the key in the lock. Alex turned the knob, and the door opened without a sound. Alex stepped inside first. Zenda followed behind Gena and Astrid.

Zenda gasped. The room looked beautiful. The Lotus Building was where the school held concerts, art shows, and meetings, and now it was decorated for the gazing ball ceremony.

Flower garlands hung from the ceiling. Thin, wooden pedestals lined the walls. On each pedestal was a small wooden box.

"The gazing balls," Alex whispered. "They must be in the boxes."

Gena and Astrid rushed to the pedestals, but Zenda approached more cautiously.

"This one has my name on it!" Astrid called out.

"Astrid, quiet!" Alex hissed.

The boxes were probably arranged alphabetically, Zenda guessed. She walked to the very last pedestal and picked up the box.

She held up her moonglow flower, which illuminated her name carefully etched into the wood:

*Zenda*

With trembling hands, Zenda tucked the moonglow flower behind her ear and opened the box lid. Tucked inside, on a cushion of silk, was her gazing ball.

It looked similar to the one Marion Rose had shown in class—a crystal sphere the size of an apple—but there was definitely something different about it. Zenda wasn't exactly sure what it was, but somehow in her soul she knew the ball was hers and hers alone, as though they were connected somehow. Zenda felt that invisible connection drawing her hand toward the ball.

Before she realized she had done it, Zenda had picked up the ball and cradled it in the palm of her hand. She held it up to catch a ray of moonlight streaming through the window.

"It's so beautiful," Zenda said, turning to

the others. Alex, Gena, and Astrid were all gazing into their boxes. They looked up at the sound of Zenda's voice.

"Zenda, don't take it out of the box!" Alex warned. "We're just here to peek, remember?"

"I just wanted a closer look," Zenda said. "It seemed to be . . . calling me almost. Do you think it has something to tell me?"

Zenda had just finished her sentence when she felt the ball tingle in her hand. A milky white mist was swirling inside the ball.

"Wait! It's doing something!" Zenda cried.

Zenda held the ball up to her face. The mist swirled like fog.

Suddenly, a bright white light flashed inside the gazing ball.

Startled, Zenda lost her hold on the smooth glass. The ball tumbled out of her fingers.

Zenda watched, horrified, as the gazing ball tumbled through the air—and crashed to the floor!

# Shattered
# Dreams

"No!" Zenda cried as the gazing ball shattered into pieces.

She fell to her knees and reached out to scoop up the broken shards. But before she could, they rose up off the ground.

Zenda froze at the sight. The pieces began to swirl in the air. Then, one by one, each piece blinked a different color, and vanished.

*One, two, three* . . . Zenda counted silently as each piece disappeared. She wanted to reach out and grab them, but something held her back. It was almost as though she were under a spell.

Finally, the last piece, the thirteenth crystal shard, vanished, and Zenda snapped back to reality.

"What am I going to do?" Zenda cried. She stood up and turned around.

Alex, Gena, and Astrid were gone.

Zenda groaned. She couldn't blame them, really.

Suddenly, Zenda was seized with panic.

Her gazing ball was gone. Vanished. Nowhere in sight. And the gazing ball ceremony was tomorrow!

The petals from her daisy crown rained to the floor as the flowers withered and died one by one.

*Calm down, Zenda,* she told herself. *Breathe. There's got to be a way to fix this.*

Except for Alex, Gena, and Astrid, nobody knew she was here. All she had to do was put the empty box back on the pedestal. When it came time to open her box during the ceremony tomorrow, she'd act surprised that it was missing. Her teachers would feel so sorry for her that they would give her a new gazing ball. Nobody would suspect her. And there's no way Alex and the others would tell— if they did, they'd be in trouble, too.

Zenda took a deep breath and rose to her feet. Everything was going to be fine. She closed the box and set it on the pedestal with trembling hands. Soon she'd be home, asleep, and this would all be behind her.

"Zenda, what are you doing here?"

Zenda spun around. Magenta White, the headmistress of the Cobalt School for Girls, stood in the doorway. She was frowning.

"I . . . I just wanted to see my gazing ball," Zenda said weakly.

Magenta clicked her tongue. "You girls today are so impatient," she said, walking briskly across the room. "Couldn't you wait until tomorrow?"

Zenda didn't know what to say. Headmistress White was intimidating under normal circumstances. She wasn't particularly tall, but her presence was larger than life. Her piercing, dark eyes and upswept, auburn hair added to the effect. And right at that moment, she seemed to tower over Zenda.

Magenta grabbed the box from Zenda's pedestal and snapped open the lid. Her frown deepened.

"Just as I thought," she said. "The gazing

balls are too delicate to be handled without proper training. You know, Zenda, there's a reason you must wait."

Ashamed, Zenda tried to look away, but Magenta held her gaze.

"How did you get in here?" she asked. "I thought I heard more than one voice."

Zenda blinked. Telling on Alex and the others wasn't going to bring her gazing ball back. She had dropped it, and she would deal with the consequences on her own. Besides, Magenta was not only the headmistress of the school, she was also Alex's mother. Alex would be in double trouble if Magenta knew the truth.

"I came alone," Zenda said, her voice shaking. "The door was open, and I was curious, so I walked in."

Magenta waited for her to say more, but Zenda kept silent. Finally, Magenta nodded.

"Very well," Magenta said. "Let's get you

home. Your parents and I have much to discuss."

Zenda felt as though her feet were made of rocks as she and Magenta walked the path toward home. She couldn't even imagine how Verbena and Vetiver were going to react. Her grandmother's words popped into her mind.

*Every choice you make has consequences.*

If only she'd paid attention to Delphina's advice—the whole advice, not just the part she'd wanted to hear. If only she hadn't listened to Alex. If only she hadn't picked up her gazing ball, everything would be fine.

But the time for "if onlys" was long over. Zenda didn't know what was ahead, but she was sure it wouldn't be good.

Verbena and Vetiver looked surprised to see Zenda enter with Magenta.

"I found Zenda in the Lotus Building," Magenta said. "There is a problem with her gazing ball."

"Oh, Zenda," Verbena said softly. Zenda could hear the disappointment in her mother's voice. "What have you done?"

Zenda didn't know what to say. Then Vetiver spoke up.

"Please go upstairs, Zenda," her father said sternly. "We'll be up to talk to you soon."

Zenda slowly climbed the stairs to her room. She closed the door, grabbed Luna, and flopped on her bed. Zenda waited anxiously, tugging at Luna's curly yarn hair. Oscar softly whined on the floor at the foot of her bed, so Zenda picked him up and set him down on the blankets. The little dog curled up at her feet.

After what seemed like hours, Zenda heard a knock on her door.

"Come in," she said.

Verbena and Vetiver walked into the room. Zenda felt a pang of regret as soon as she saw them. Vetiver's long gray hair was usually held back in a neat ponytail, but a few strands had come loose, and his normally calm face looked pained. And Verbena, usually full of energy—like a bright bird, Zenda had often thought—looked pale and tired. Vetiver sat on the edge of the bed while Verbena paced across the floor.

"How are you feeling?" her father asked.

"I'm not sure," Zenda said, smiling weakly. "How much trouble am I in?"

Usually Zenda's attempts at humor softened her parents during tense times. But now neither of them even smiled.

"Just like Delphina," Verbena muttered. "So impetuous."

Vetiver sighed and straightened his glasses. "You *are* a lot like my mother was, Zenda," he said. "I always admired her courage and free spirit. But this was a very foolish thing to do. You're twelve years old now. You should know better."

For the first time that night, Zenda felt tears sting her eyes.

"I just wanted to take a look," she said. "I

didn't think anything bad would happen."

"You need to know that it's not okay to lie to us, or to go off on your own without telling us," Verbena said.

"I know," Zenda said sincerely. "I'm sorry."

"We think you should spend the next week thinking about that," Verbena continued. "You'll be on restriction here, helping us in the gardens."

Zenda nodded. One week of restriction wasn't so bad. She could handle it. But there was still one thing that worried her.

"What about my gazing ball ceremony?" she asked.

Zenda's parents exchanged glances.

"You won't be going to the gazing ball ceremony tomorrow," Vetiver said softly. "Not without your gazing ball."

A feeling of dread filled the pit of Zenda's stomach. "But everyone on Azureblue gets a gazing ball before they turn thirteen. Can't they just give me a new one?"

Zenda had doubts as soon as she said the words. The gazing ball had been specially made for her when she was born. Replacing it couldn't be easy—but she was hopeful.

"It's not that simple, Zenda," Verbena said, confirming her fears. "There is no way to make a replacement. You will have to put your gazing ball back together yourself."

"But how?" Zenda asked, panic rising in her voice. "I saw the pieces vanish!"

"I know it sounds incredible," Vetiver said. "Believe it or not, this is not the first time that a gazing ball has been broken. There is a way to find the missing pieces, but you will have to do that on your own."

"What do you mean?" Zenda asked.

Vetiver and Verbena looked at each other again. Zenda knew more bad news was coming. Finally, Vetiver spoke.

"You won't be going to gazing ball class with the rest of the girls in school," he said. "The other girls will be studying their gazing balls during the class. The balls will reveal the musings one by one, and Marion Rose will help the girls explore them. But you don't have a gazing ball to study."

Zenda couldn't believe it. "But can't Marion Rose help me, too?"

"No one can find the missing pieces for you, Zenda," Vetiver said. "You'll have to do it on your own—wherever the journey takes you."

"You won't be completely alone, Zenda," Verbena said gently. "Your father and I are here to support you."

"This isn't fair," Zenda cried, suddenly feeling angry. "I know I made a mistake, but I shouldn't have to miss the ceremony and everything!"

Zenda fell back on her bed and buried her face in her pillows. Through her sobs, she heard the soft footsteps of her parents as they left the room and closed the door.

*Hopeless!*

This is the most unfair thing that has ever happened to anyone on Azureblue! I know it was wrong to sneak into the Lotus Room with Alex. But it's not like I committed some horrible crime or something. Besides, the whole thing was Alex's idea.

And I didn't mean to break the gazing ball! That weird light flashed, and I got startled. It's almost like the gazing ball jumped out of my hands on purpose.

And now I can't go to the gazing ball ceremony.

That's the worst, most horrible punishment I could ever imagine. When I don't show up, everyone will know that something is wrong.

*There is no way I am going to school today.*

*V & V will have to understand.*

*I just can't face everybody. I can't!!!*

———⦿———

Zenda had been writing ever since the morning bells had roused her from a fitful sleep. She kept writing, ignoring the breakfast chimes completely.

Finally, she heard a soft knock on her door. Zenda sighed and closed the book.

"Come in," Zenda said.

Vetiver entered, carrying a tray with a bowl of creamed wheat and a glass of mango-kiwi juice, Zenda's favorite. He set the tray on Zenda's desk.

"I know this is hard for you, starshine," he said. "But you'll feel better soon, I promise. Now come on and eat your creamed wheat. I put some strawberries in it for you."

Zenda sat up. The hot cereal did smell good. Vetiver had sprinkled some cinnamon on it, too.

"Thanks, Dad," Zenda said. "But I'm not going to school today. I just can't!"

Vetiver stood silent for a moment. Finally, he cleared his throat.

"You know, when I said you reminded me of Delphina, I meant it," he said. "Your grandmother was not afraid of anything. I know the idea of going to school today might be a little scary, but Delphina would have done it. She would have held her head up high."

Vetiver left the room and closed the door.

Thorns! Her father had said the one thing he knew would get through to her. He was right. Delphina never cared much what anyone thought of her. She wouldn't be afraid to go to school one bit.

"All right," Zenda said, picking up Luna and looking her right in the eyes. "I'm going. But if I die of embarrassment, you'll have to go live with Camille."

This morning, Mykal was waiting by the door to walk to school with Zenda. She could tell from the sad look in his eyes that he knew what had happened.

Zenda felt like turning right around and going back inside. If Mykal thought she was flighty before, he probably wanted nothing to do with her now.

But something in Mykal's eyes told her he didn't feel that way.

"I guess you know," she said.

"Your mom and dad told me," he said. "Because of the party and all. I told them I didn't want to have one. It wouldn't be the same without you there."

Zenda couldn't believe how sweet Mykal was being. She felt like crying all over again.

"You don't have to do that for me," she replied. "You deserve a party. It's not like you went and broke your gazing ball."

Mykal grinned. "Hey, you never know. I'm pretty clumsy. I'll probably trip and it'll go flying. Or maybe I'll sneeze all over it."

Zenda found herself giggling in spite of her misery. "Hey, maybe that's one of your musings: 'He who sneezes never pleases.'"

Mykal laughed. "Or maybe it'll be: 'The key to happiness lies in a single sneeze.'"

They reached the Commons, and Zenda's smile faded. Mykal had been really nice about things—in fact, he'd been nicer to her than he had ever been before. But the girls in school were another matter.

Mykal paused at the path that led to his school, the Cobalt School for Boys. "See you later," he said quietly. "Don't worry. It'll be okay." He smiled encouragingly, then ran ahead to catch up with a group of boys.

Zenda gave a weak wave and walked toward the girls' school. She saw the towering willow tree and remembered how spooky it had seemed the night before.

*It was an omen,* Zenda thought. *Old Man Willow was telling me to go home. I should have listened.*

Camille ran up and threw her arms around Zenda.

"Oh, Zenda!" she cried. "Is it true? Did you really break your gazing ball?"

"How did you know?" Zenda asked anxiously.

Camille motioned toward a group of girls by the door of the Sage Building. Alex White stood in the middle while the others leaned in, taking in her every word.

"Alex said her mother found you in the Lotus Room last night," Camille said. "She told everybody."

Zenda felt like screaming.

"If it wasn't for Alex, I wouldn't have been there in the first place!" Zenda snapped. "I could have told her mother, but I didn't. Now I wish I had."

"No, you don't," Camille said. "I know you. You're too nice for that."

Zenda moaned and leaned against the tree.

"I can't go in there! Everyone must think I'm such a loser."

Camille shook her head. "I don't think so. They just feel bad that you're going to miss the ceremony tonight."

Zenda sighed. Having people feel sorry for you was just as bad as having them think you were a loser—maybe worse.

"Come on, Zenda," Camille urged, grabbing Zenda's hand. "We're going to be late."

Camille led Zenda to her learning station. Alex, Gena, and Astrid walked past, purposefully avoiding Zenda's gaze. As they walked away, Zenda heard Alex whisper, "I guess Zenda's amazing gift wasn't good enough to fix her gazing ball." Gena and Astrid burst into giggles.

An angry response flashed through Zenda's mind, but before she could speak, she felt a sharp pinch on top of her head. She gingerly reached up and lifted off her flower crown. The delicate crown of violets she had woven this morning had transformed into a crown of tiny red roses peppered with sharp, angry-looking thorns. Zenda tossed the crown aside. She didn't feel like she belonged with the other girls, anyway. What point was there in wearing her crown?

The morning passed by as slowly as a slug. As usual, the girls spent the morning working on their independent projects. After lunch, however, the day became more formal. The afternoon started out with some kind of plant-related class, like botany or herbology. Plants were considered so important on Azureblue that the plant sciences were taught all through high school.

Then, after plant science, the students received instruction on a subject, such as music or art, which rotated every six months. But the next six months were special. Now after plant science, students who were twelve years old went to gazing ball class instead. Every student, boy or girl, completed the gazing ball study.

*Every student except for me*, Zenda thought miserably, poking at the ball of clay in her hand.

Finally, the lunch bells chimed. Marion Rose walked to Zenda's learning station and pulled her aside.

"I know your parents have told you this," the teacher said softly. "From now on, you'll be going home before gazing ball class begins. Normally you'd have botany class first, but that's canceled today. The other girls will have a special class today, right after lunch. You can go home now if you want to."

Zenda nodded and tried to answer, but the words got stuck in her throat. It was hard to believe this was really happening.

"I know how hard this is for you, Zenda," Marion Rose said. "But I also know you'll be able to find those gazing ball pieces on your own. If anyone can do it, it will be my most creative student."

Zenda couldn't help smiling at her teacher. Marion Rose had a way about her that just made you feel good about yourself.

"I'll see you tomorrow, Zenda," the teacher continued. "I'm sure it will be a better day."

Going home early sounded good to Zenda. As she waved good-bye to Camille and left the building, she thought she could feel the eyes of every girl watching her. She swore she heard whispers behind her as she left.

Back home, her parents were eating lunch at the long wooden table in the sun room with the staff from Azureblue Karmaceuticals. The midday meal was always a big event. No one seemed surprised to see her home early. Marion Rose must have sent a message on to her parents, Zenda guessed.

Zenda accepted a plate of salad from her mother and poked at the greens in silence while the others talked and laughed. Finally, she was left alone with Verbena and Vetiver.

Zenda's parents began to clean up and Zenda, out of habit, stayed to help them. Her father washed the dishes, Zenda dried them, and Verbena flitted from cabinet to cabinet like a hummingbird, putting everything back in order. Verbena had dreamed of being a dancer when she was a child. After she got her gazing ball and discovered she had the gift of *kani*, she had decided to become a karmacist instead. But she had never really stopped dancing.

The routine felt familiar, but usually Zenda and her parents talked or joked while cleaning up together. Today, however, they moved in silence. Zenda's gazing ball disaster had cast a shadow over everything. Zenda knew how disappointed her parents were and she could hardly stand it. When the last dish was put away, Zenda started to slip out of the room. But Vetiver put a hand on her shoulder.

"I'm glad you went to school this morning," he said. "I'm proud of you; I know it was hard."

"Thanks," Zenda said. "And I've been thinking. About the gazing ball. I mean, what do I have to do to get it back?"

"Maybe we should sit down," Verbena said. Her voice had the same edge of disappointment that it had the night before.

"What now?" Zenda asked, sinking into her seat.

Verbena sighed. "Getting back your gazing ball isn't so simple, Zenda. In fact, we're not sure how you're supposed to get it back."

"But I thought this has happened before?" Zenda asked, puzzled.

"It has," her father replied. "But gazing balls are tricky. They're different for every person. You will have to figure it out on your own."

Zenda rose from her seat, frustrated. "But how? Am I supposed to be searching for it somewhere? Do I get a map or something?"

"The answer will come to you," Vetiver said gently. "You just have to be patient."

"But I thought—the ceremony is

tonight—I thought maybe—" Zenda felt her frustration growing.

"Zenda, there's no quick fix for this," Verbena said, shaking her head. "Why don't you meditate for a while and see if an answer comes to you? That's what I do when I have a problem to solve."

Zenda had often wondered how her mother could meditate when she never seemed to sit still. Meditation wasn't Zenda's strongest skill, but she didn't know what else to do.

"Thanks," Zenda muttered. She left the kitchen and walked back outside. She didn't feel quite right without a flower crown on her head. She fashioned a simple crown from green clover and then headed for the family meditation room.

Zenda perched on a pile of purple silk pillows, crossed her legs, and closed her eyes.

*Where are the pieces of my gazing ball? Where are the pieces of my gazing ball? Where are the pieces of my gazing ball?*

Zenda repeated the mantra in her mind over and over and over. But the only image that came to her was the vision of the gazing ball pieces as they vanished into thin air, one by one.

Vetiver found her slumped on the cushions with her chin in her hands.

"I thought you might need some help," he said, handing her a clay mug. "This rosemary tea will help clear your mind."

"It's no use," Zenda said, taking a sip. "Meditation is just making my mind more crowded."

Vetiver smiled. "How about some *sela*? That always works for me."

Like most children on Azureblue, Zenda had been taught the ancient *sela* exercises since she could walk. The movements were said to strengthen the body and the mind at the same time. Vetiver was particularly good at it. Zenda marveled at the way he could twist his lanky arms and legs together like vines.

Vetiver clasped his hands together,

extending his elbows out to each side. Then he lifted his right leg and placed the bottom of his foot against his left knee.

"The tree pose is one of my favorites," he said. "While one part of your brain is concentrating on balance, the other is free to solve challenges."

Zenda stood next to her father and copied the pose. She closed her eyes.

But all she could think of was the tall willow tree, looming above her, warning her of what was to come . . .

"No use," Zenda said, her eyes springing open. "I think I'll go to my room for a while."

Her father didn't open his eyes, but he nodded to let Zenda know he'd heard her.

Zenda took the tea to her room and sat on her bed.

"What do you know, Luna?" she asked her doll. "Can you tell me how to get back my gazing ball?"

Luna just smiled back.

Zenda sighed and took out her notebook.

---

*Everyone says the answer is inside me. Then why is it so hard to find? Am I asking the wrong questions?*

---

Zenda closed the book and wandered over to her dresser, touching the glass bottles of body elixirs one by one. There was one for Relaxation, one for Meditation, another for Exhilaration . . .

Zenda's hand rested on the bottle marked *Inspiration.* She uncapped the bottle and sprayed some on her neck and arms. The scent of sweet pea and grapefruit filled the air.

Oscar padded into the room, happily wagging his tail.

"Doesn't that smell good, Oscar?" Zenda

asked. "Let's see if it works. Come on, I'll take you for a walk. Maybe some inspiration will come to me then."

Oscar followed Zenda downstairs, but her enthusiasm fizzled out as soon as she reached the front porch.

*What's the use?* she thought, sinking down on the porch swing. *This is hopeless!*

Verbena walked onto the porch and pulled Zenda off the swing.

"I think you need to dance," she said. "Close your eyes and take a deep breath."

Zenda made a face. "How is this going to help, exactly?" she asked.

"You'll see," Verbena said.

Reluctantly, Zenda closed her eyes.

"Now listen to your heartbeat. Listen to it echo in your ears."

Zenda focused.

*Thump. Thump. Thump.* The sound started off faintly, but the more Zenda listened, the louder it became.

"Now move with your heartbeat." Verbena's voice sounded distant. "Move your feet. Move your hands. Move your head."

Zenda moved, stiffly at first. But soon, she found a groove. Her heartbeat sounded just like the drummers who performed in the Village Commons on festival nights. She could dance to the drums; why not dance to the beat of her own body?

Zenda danced across the porch and inside the house.

*Thump. Thump. Thump.*

She opened her eyes and bounded up the stairs, moving faster with each step. When she reached her bedroom, Zenda let loose.

Zenda moved faster and faster now. As she twirled around the room, she felt suddenly free.

*I can do this*, she realized. *I can find my gazing ball. I'm not sure how. But I'll find a way.*

Suddenly, her rhythm was interrupted by another sound—the sound of pipes and flutes.

Zenda stopped and looked out the window. It was sundown. The gazing ball ceremony was beginning.

And she wasn't there.

Suddenly deflated, she flopped down onto her bed.

*A Solution . . .
with a Catch*

The next day at school, everyone had their gazing balls with them, kept safely in their wooden boxes. Zenda tried to tune out all of the talk as the girls chatted about the ceremony the night before.

Camille hadn't said a word about the ceremony, and Zenda knew her friend was trying to spare her feelings. But deep inside, Zenda wanted to find out what had happened. She wanted to see Camille's gazing ball and find out if Camille had learned any secrets.

"Come on, Cam," Zenda said as they ate lunch under the willow tree. "I really want to know what happened last night."

Camille looked relieved to hear Zenda's request. "I've been dying to talk to you about it," she said, her face glowing with excitement. "It was beautiful. First, Headmistress White called our names one by one and gave us our gazing balls. Then a member of each person's family read a list of wishes for our future."

"Who read yours?" Zenda asked.

"My mom," Camille replied. "She wished that I would be able to follow my dreams, whatever they are. I almost cried."

Zenda felt like crying, too. She wondered what wishes Verbena and Vetiver would have had for her. Right now, they probably wished they had a daughter who didn't go around breaking her gazing ball.

When it came time for botany class, Zenda felt a sense of relief. Normally, she dragged her feet to the class; the facts and figures spouted by Dr. Ledger seemed to take all the life out of the beautiful plants she knew. But at least she'd have something to listen to besides the whisperings of excited girls.

Everything about Dr. Ledger was neat. He wore a perfectly pressed white lab coat, as always, which contrasted with his dark skin. His close-cropped gray hair and wire-rimmed glasses made him look like a very serious person, which he was.

"Today we will begin our study of seed

germination," Dr. Ledger began when the girls were settled into their chairs. "It's very appropriate, I think. Your gazing ball ceremony yesterday planted the seed for a time of personal growth. As I always say, people and plants have much in common."

Zenda sighed quietly and slumped in her seat. When Dr. Ledger started talking about people and plants, you knew it was going to be a long lesson.

"Now then," he said. "I'm excited to say that we'll be experimenting with seed germination right here in the classroom. Each of you will need a partner to work with."

Zenda sat up and beamed at Camille. She and her friend always worked together. But Dr. Ledger had other thoughts.

"I'll be assigning partners today," he said. "Just as different plants grow together in one space, different people need to learn to grow together."

Dr. Ledger read off the list of partners.

Finally, Zenda heard, "Alexandra, you will be Zenda's partner."

Zenda couldn't believe it. She had been avoiding Alex ever since the night she broke the gazing ball. She was still hurt and angry that Alex had told everyone in school what had happened. And then there was that mean comment. It made her so mad.

Zenda quickly raised a hand to her flower crown. The circle of buttercups she had woven this morning hadn't sprouted thorns or anything—yet. She took a deep breath.

When Alex approached her table, she acted like nothing had happened.

"Hey, Zenda," she said. "Seed germination. Sounds like fun, doesn't it?"

"Sure," Zenda said sullenly.

Dr. Ledger set a vial of seeds on the table in front of them.

"You all will be growing talus flowers," he announced, "some of the most delicate flowers in Azureblue. It takes a great deal of care and attention before each flower reaches maturity in six months."

Dr. Ledger walked to the front of the class and continued talking about the talus flower. As soon as he started, Zenda felt Alex nudge her.

"Finally," Alex whispered. "I've been meaning to talk to you. Thanks for not ratting me out to my mom."

Zenda shrugged. That was something, at least.

Alex leaned closer, and Zenda realized how much she looked like her mother. She had the same chestnut hair and bright, dark eyes.

"I think I have a solution to your problem," Alex continued. Then she reached into the silk pouch that she wore around her waist and pulled out an old, tattered book. *A History of Gazing Balls* was stamped into the cover in gold.

"I got this from my mom's private library, where all her important books are kept,"

Alex said. "It's all about gazing balls. You're never going to guess what's in it!"

"Unless my gazing ball is in there somewhere, I'm not interested," Zenda said.

"Trust me, this is good," Alex said. "There's a ritual in here for putting the pieces of a broken gazing ball back together."

Zenda jumped a little in her seat.

"Are you serious?" she asked.

Alex nodded. "It just takes an hour, and you'll get your gazing ball back."

"Great!" Zenda said. "So how do you do it?"

Alex bit her bottom lip. "Well, there's kind of a catch," she admitted. "The ritual is sort of . . . forbidden."

Zenda's happiness evaporated. "What do you mean, sort of forbidden?"

"Well, really, *really* forbidden, actually," Alex said. "To do the ritual, you need an azura orchid."

Zenda gasped. The azura orchid was one

of the rarest plants on the planet. It was said to possess mysterious powers. For that reason, only trained karmacists were allowed to even handle it.

"You must be crazy," Zenda said. "I want to get my gazing ball back, but there's no way I'm going to perform a forbidden ritual. Besides, where would I get my hands on an azura orchid?"

Alex grinned. "Easy," she replied. "Just steal one from your parents!"

# The Forbidden Flower

Zenda was too stunned to reply. It was true: Her parents were among the few people on the planet licensed to grow azura orchids. But ever since she was a little girl, she had been told how dangerous they were, and she was never allowed to go near them. Verbena and Vetiver kept them locked in a special room in the main greenhouse.

"Is that the only way?" Zenda finally asked.

Alex nodded. "But think of it, Zenda. By tonight, you'll have your gazing ball. You can put the orchid back before your parents realize it's gone."

Zenda shook her head. "I don't know," she said. "I feel bad enough about sneaking out the other night. But stealing from my parents . . ."

Alex rolled her eyes. "It's not really stealing, is it? I mean, you're all in the same family. How can you steal from yourself?"

Zenda forgot that it was Alex herself who

had used the word "stealing" in the first place. In fact, she started to think that Alex was making sense.

Sure, for a brief moment yesterday, she had felt that she could find the gazing ball on her own. But who knows how long that would take? She had been asking the universe for an answer, and now Alex was dropping one in her lap. For all she knew, using the orchid and performing the ritual was what she was supposed to do.

Dr. Ledger's crisp voice interrupted her thoughts. "Zenda and Alexandra, I hope you two are paying attention."

"Yes, sir," the girls replied in unison. Dr. Ledger turned back to the class, and Alex whispered in Zenda's ear.

"If you decide to do it, come to my tree house at sundown. I'll be waiting for you."

Alex and Zenda finished the class in silence. After class, the other girls headed for gazing ball study, and Zenda went home.

Vetiver suggested Zenda come help in the gardens for a while.

"I think the roses miss you," he said with a smile.

Zenda's thoughts were too anxious to think about plants, but she didn't know what else to do. She followed her father into the rose garden.

The plants looked much healthier than they had just two days before. Some of the flowers were still blue, but Zenda had to admit they looked kind of pretty among the red flowers.

"Hello there," Zenda said, placing her hands on a rosebush. "How are you doing today?"

Zenda's mind reached out toward the plant, trying to make contact . . . but the rosebush was silent.

"That's weird," Zenda said, frowning. "Nothing happened." She opened her eyes and stepped back.

A strange thought popped into Zenda's mind. *Maybe it knows what I'm thinking of doing.*

*Maybe it doesn't want to talk to me.*

Then Zenda felt her father's hand on her shoulder.

"Plants are very sensitive to the moods of their growers," he said gently. "Perhaps it senses how upset you are about breaking your gazing ball. I wouldn't worry. When you're feeling better, your gift will return."

Zenda sighed with relief. Of course. That must be it. And the only way to fix it was to get her gazing ball back as soon as possible. Alex's forbidden ritual might be her only chance.

"The herb garden can use some weeding," Vetiver said. "Why don't we try that for a while?"

Zenda nodded and followed her father. As she pulled weed after weed from the dirt, she turned the argument over in her mind.

*It's not really stealing,* Alex had said. The more she repeated it, the more convinced she became.

"Hi, Zenda."

Zenda turned to see Camille standing there. Her friend waved.

"I thought I'd come and see how you were," she said. "It must be hard for you, not going to gazing ball class and all."

Zenda shrugged, not wanting Camille to see how much it really upset her. "I'm sure I'll be going to class soon," she replied. "I have a feeling I'm going to get my gazing ball back before you know it."

Camille plopped down in the dirt next to Zenda. "Oh, that's great! Class isn't the same without you. Although it is pretty fun. Just today I—"

Camille stopped, not wanting to hurt Zenda's feelings.

"That's okay, Cam," Zenda said. "I'm all right. I meant it when I said you could talk to me about your gazing ball."

Camille nodded. Then she took off her backpack and pulled out a small wooden box. Zenda knew just what was inside.

Camille opened the lid to reveal her gazing ball. A pale, pink mist swirled inside.

"At first the ball was clear, but the mist appeared this morning," she said. "And then the mist formed words. Marion Rose said it was my first musing. Can you believe it?"

"So is that how it happens?" Zenda asked. "The musings just pop up?"

Camille nodded. "Marion Rose says the first one comes pretty quickly. Now that I have my first musing, I'm supposed to study it for a while, and think about what it means to me. When the gazing ball thinks I'm ready, I'll get my second musing."

Zenda felt a quick pang of jealousy, but her excitement for her friend won out.

"What did it say?"

"*You cannot imagine without a dream in your heart,*" Camille said. "Isn't that beautiful?"

"Wow," Zenda said, and the jealousy returned.

At that moment, she made up her mind.

She would not wait around while everyone else got their musings. She would take the orchid, go to Alexandra's, and get her gazing ball back tonight.

Zenda gave Camille a hug. "Don't worry," she said. "I'll see you in class soon."

Zenda waited until after dinner to carry out her plan. She told Verbena and Vetiver that she was going to try to communicate with plants in the greenhouse. Her parents, of course, thought that was wonderful.

"Your father told me you had a little block this afternoon," Verbena said. "It happens to all of us from time to time. But you're doing just the right thing by trying to work it out. I'm proud of you."

Zenda felt guilty, but shook off the feeling.

*They'll be even more proud when I come home tonight with my gazing ball,* she told herself.

Zenda walked to the main greenhouse. The huge, glass-walled building had a curved roof. The structure had always reminded her of a giant loaf of bread.

Rows and rows of plants lined the greenhouse, plants that needed extra warmth and light. Zenda slowly walked down the aisle to the sealed room in which the azura orchids were kept.

Getting into the room would be easy. Her parents were so trusting that they kept a ring of keys in plain sight, on a hook on the wall. Deep down, Zenda knew that this was partly because the azura orchid had such a dangerous reputation and no Azurean would dream of handling it.

*But you're not just any Azurean*, Zenda told herself. *Your parents are licensed karmacists, and they've been training you since you were born. Nothing bad is going to happen.*

She found the key and walked to the door, then stopped.

Ever since she could remember, she had been told never to go near this room, and she had obeyed without question. She didn't even know what an azura orchid looked like. What if it was some kind of monstrous thing that ate humans? Or maybe it was poisonous just to look at it?

*Don't be silly*, Zenda scolded herself. *It's just a plant. Open the door and look.*

Zenda put the key in the lock. She slowly opened the door and peeked in.

A dozen clay pots sat on a table in the center of the room. Each pot was covered with a clear glass dome. And, inside each dome, was an azura orchid. A faint sweet, spicy smell greeted Zenda as she entered the room.

*The orchid's smell must be powerful if it can penetrate through the dome*, Zenda realized. But what made the orchid so dangerous?

She cautiously stepped closer. Each orchid rose from the dirt on a pale, green stem. Three delicate, lacy petals, the light blue color of a clear early morning sky, framed a tube-shaped petal in the center. There were no sharp teeth or giant horns; no oozing toxic slime. The orchids looked fragile and not at all dangerous.

Zenda took a deep breath and picked up one of the plants, half expecting some kind of alarm to go off. Nothing happened.

She let out her breath and tiptoed toward the door. She closed and locked the door behind her.

"Don't worry," she told the orchid, slipping a cloth over the glass case. "I just need you for a little while. Then I'll get you back home safely."

And then she stepped out into the dusk.

# The Orchid's Power

The setting sun streaked the blue sky with brilliant purple brushstrokes as Zenda walked to Alex's house. Alex and her mother lived just a little bit north of the girls' school, so Zenda didn't have far to go.

Normally, Zenda would have noticed the purple sunset, or the song of the sparrows as they headed to their nests for the night, or the sound of nearby Crystal Creek as the water gently trickled over the stones.

But tonight, the scent of the azura orchid seemed to command all of Zenda's senses as it seeped through the glass dome. The scent reminded her of so many things at once, and yet of nothing at all that she could recognize. Its spicy sweetness tickled her nose. Her thoughts were focused on the orchid, and it took all of her discipline not to lift the cover right there on the path to take a close-up look at the plant.

As Zenda walked, she noticed something strange. Instead of rustling at her in greeting, like they normally did, the branches of the trees seemed to be shrinking back from her. Zenda thought of the rosebush earlier.

*Do they know what I'm planning to do?* Zenda wondered. It didn't matter. Zenda had made up her mind, and she wasn't going to stop now. She broke into a run, anxious to get to Alex's and start the ritual.

"The sooner I get there, the sooner this will all be over," Zenda muttered as she ran.

Minutes later, she arrived at a tall, box-shaped house with a fresh coat of white paint. To Zenda, the house seemed cool and proper—just like Headmistress White. Zenda walked around back to the only unusual-looking thing on the White's property: the wooden tree house nestled in the gnarled branches of an old chestnut tree.

Climbing up the ladder to the tree house and holding the orchid at the same time wasn't easy, but Zenda managed. She pulled herself up onto the platform.

A circle of beeswax candlesticks in glass holders lit up the tiny room. Alex, Gena, and Astrid sat cross-legged outside the circle. Alex held the book about gazing balls on her lap.

"I knew you'd come," Alex said smugly. "Now we can start."

Gena and Astrid exchanged glances, and Zenda realized they were terrified. Astrid's face was paler than ever, and Gena was twirling a strand of her black hair around and around her finger.

"Is that the—the orchid?" Gena asked nervously.

Zenda removed the cloth that covered the glass dome, and the girls gasped.

"She really got it," Astrid breathed.

Alex grinned. "Perfect!" she said. "Zenda, take the orchid and step into the circle."

Zenda stepped over the candles and sat in the center of the circle, setting the orchid in front of her.

"And now for the ritual," Alex said,

opening the book.

But Gena stopped her. "I don't know, Alex," she said. "I mean, it seemed like a good idea, but . . ."

" . . . maybe we shouldn't do it," Astrid finished for her. "I didn't think Zenda would really get the orchid. What if something bad happens?"

To her surprise, Zenda didn't feel nervous at all. Instead, she felt impatient for the ritual to start—and annoyed with Gena and Astrid for slowing things down.

"Nothing bad is going to happen as long as you two stay out of the way," Zenda snapped. As soon as the words came out, she regretted them. It didn't sound like her at all.

"Sorry," she said. "I didn't mean it. I guess I just want to get this over with and get back my gazing ball."

Gena and Astrid frowned. Then Alex jumped in.

"Everything's going to be fine," she told

them. "As long as we follow the book exactly, nothing will go wrong. Okay?"

The two girls didn't reply, but they both nodded.

"All right," Zenda said. "Let's do this!"

"Let us begin," Alex said in an imposing and mysterious voice. Then she recited the first lines of the ritual.

*"Legend are the powers of the azura orchid. Precious is the scent that rises from its essence. May all present swear to use this power wisely, or suffer the sting of a thousand thorns."*

Alex held up her right hand. "I do swear," she said solemnly.

"Me, too!" Zenda said quickly.

Gena and Astrid looked horrified.

"It's your turn," Alex hissed.

"The sting of a thousand thorns?" Astrid whispered.

"I knew this was a bad idea," Gena moaned.

Alex rolled her eyes. "Don't be silly!" she said in her normal voice. "We are using the power of the orchid wisely. We're getting Zenda's gazing ball back, aren't we? Just go ahead and swear."

Gena sighed. "I swear," she mumbled.

"I guess I do, too," Astrid said. Tears welled up in her eyes.

"Can we get on with this?" Zenda asked.

"Of course," Alex said. "Now I just have to find my place . . ." She flipped through the pages. "I can't find it!"

"It's a sign," Gena said. "We should stop right now."

Astrid began to cry. "I want to go home," she sobbed.

Zenda had had enough. She reached out of the circle and grabbed the book.

"I'll find it," she said.

But Alex wouldn't let go. "You can't do it," she said, her voice rising. "I have to be the one to do it!"

"Says who?" Zenda asked. "You don't even know where to look in the book."

"I do, too!" Alex whined. "Just give me a minute. Don't be so impatient!"

"This is ridiculous," Zenda said. "I should have figured you'd mess things up, just like you messed things up the other night."

"Me? You were the one who dropped your gazing ball," Alex shot back.

Both Gena and Astrid were crying now.

"Stop fighting! Please!" Gena begged.

At that moment, Zenda felt inexplicably drawn to the orchid. She stared at its lacy blue petals. In the next instant, words popped into Zenda's brain.

*STOP NOW.*

Zenda froze. She had heard the words loud and clear, yet she knew that they hadn't been spoken aloud. No, she was sure that, somehow, they had come from the orchid.

Wherever the words had come from, their message snapped Zenda out of her impatience for a moment. She had a sudden realization.

"This isn't right," Zenda said. As she

spoke, the petals from her buttercup crown tumbled to the floor, dried up and dead. The stems felt like brittle twigs on her head.

"I told you, I'm going to find it!" Alex snapped.

"No, I don't mean that," Zenda said. "I mean how we're acting. It's not normal. I shouldn't be so upset that you lost your place. Gena and Astrid shouldn't be crying. Look at them, they're hysterical —"

"That's ridiculous!" Alex interrupted. "You're just chickening out. I knew you were too afraid to go through with this!"

"That's fine with me," Gena said through her tears. "Let's stop the ritual. Please!"

Whatever clarity Zenda had felt before vanished immediately. Zenda's old impatience came rushing back.

"No!" Zenda cried. "Let's finish it. I'm not afraid, and I'll prove it!"

Zenda reached across the circle to grab the book away from Alex. Her elbow hit the azura orchid, knocking the plant on its side.

The glass dome shattered into pieces.

Immediately, the smell of the azura orchid filled the tree house. The faint, sweet, spicy smell had been pleasant, but at full force it was something altogether different. Zenda could almost feel the scent clinging to her hair, seeping into her clothes, settling in her pores. She tried to breathe, and the scent filled her lungs.

"Do you break *everything* you touch?" Alex yelled.

"I knew it!" Zenda cried, panic swarming over her. "The orchid did this to us. We've got to find something to cover it with. We've got to get it back to the greenhouse before—"

"Forget it," Alex said. "You've really messed things up, Zenda. I'm going to get my mother. I'm going to tell her you stole the orchid and brought it here. I'm not going to take the blame for this!"

Before Zenda could stop her, Alex scrambled down the tree house ladder.

Out of
Control

"Come back here!" Zenda yelled. She turned to Gena and Astrid. "Where's her mother? In the house?"

Gena shook her head. "She's at the school tonight," she answered through her sobs.

Zenda grabbed the orchid and started down the ladder. She had to catch Alex. She just had to. And then she'd convince her that they could still return the orchid safely. No one would ever have to know.

As Zenda's foot touched the grass, she felt something hit the top of her head.

"Ow!" Zenda said, rubbing her head. She looked up. "Gena? Astrid?"

A shower of chestnuts fell from the tree branches, raining on her body. Clusters of the nuts hung from every branch. She quickly dodged out of the way as more showered down.

If Zenda hadn't been in such a hurry, she might have stopped to wonder why the tree was suddenly loaded with ripe chestnuts, and far too many at that. But all she could think about was getting to Alexandra before it was too late.

Clutching the orchid, Zenda ran down the path, her heart pounding. The flower's scent was overwhelming, but she didn't slow down.

Zenda ran toward a small maple sapling. As she passed by, Zenda watched, amazed, as the tree began to grow at super speed, its branches extending far over the path.

She ran past a wild rosebush. Almost immediately, hundreds of closed buds on the plant swelled and burst open into pale pink flowers.

"What's happening?" Zenda cried.

She ran past a field of dandelions. The yellow flowers faded to brown and then transformed into soft white puffs in seconds. The puffs scattered on the breeze, making the field look as though it was caught in a snow flurry.

Zenda stopped and looked around her,

transfixed. Every nearby plant was growing at a rapid rate. She stared as the pink blossoms of an apple tree transformed into tiny green apples in front of her eyes.

"The orchid," Zenda breathed. It had affected the girls' behavior, and now it was affecting the plants, too. She had to do something, fast. She couldn't wait.

Zenda's mind raced for an answer. The Cobalt School for Girls was just down the path. She could take it to Headmistress White and explain everything. She would know what to do.

To the left was a small wooden bridge that crossed Crystal Creek. The sound of flowing water sparked an idea.

She could throw the orchid in the creek. The water would stop the orchid's scent, and it would float harmlessly downstream. No one would ever have to know she was involved. Everything would be solved in just seconds.

She ran to the bridge and raised her arm, ready to throw the orchid into the water.

But a strong hand grabbed Zenda's wrist.

"Don't do it!" an unfamiliar voice commanded.

*Persuaja*

Zenda turned to find a tall woman standing over her. Startled, she surrendered the orchid. The woman quickly placed it in a metal box and snapped the lid shut.

"I'm sorry to have frightened you," she said. "But I couldn't let you throw the orchid into the creek. The scent would have escaped into the water, contaminating the water supply."

Zenda wasn't sure if she should feel relieved or afraid. She thought she knew everyone in the village, but this woman didn't look familiar at all. She had long, black hair that cascaded down her back. Covering her shoulders was a long, purple cloak that seemed to change color slightly as she moved. A mass of strange-looking amulets and crystals dangled from chains around her neck. And her face—well, Zenda couldn't exactly guess how old she might be. Her skin wasn't wrinkled, yet there was something ancient about her eyes, which were the color of the midnight sky.

Who was this woman? And why did she want the orchid? Zenda tried to speak, but she found that the woman's very presence seemed to silence her.

To Zenda's surprise, the woman seemed to read her thoughts.

"My name is Persuaja," she said. "I'd like you to tell me how you came to be holding an azura orchid, if you don't mind. But first—"

Persuaja reached into a purple pouch she wore around her neck. Her hands jingled as they moved, and Zenda realized that she wore bracelets on each arm. Countless keys of all shapes and sizes dangled from the bracelets.

Persuaja took a small vial out of the pouch and waved it under Zenda's nose.

"Breathe deeply, young lady," she said. "It's an antidote to the orchid."

Zenda did as instructed—she was too much in awe of Persuaja not to—and a clean scent wafted up. The effect was immediate; Zenda felt suddenly calmer and clear-headed. Zenda found that she now had the courage to speak.

"How did you know I was here?" Zenda asked.

Persuaja smiled. "It's quite simple, actually," she said. "The azura orchid created a powerful disturbance in the astral plane. I followed the energy right to you."

"So you must be—" Only psychics could travel in the astral plane. Zenda had never actually met a psychic before. The gifts of a psychic were even rarer than the gift of *kani*.

Persuaja nodded. "Yes. You are right, Zenda. But perhaps now you can tell me your story."

"I . . . I was trying to get back my gazing ball," Zenda said. "There was a ritual . . . and my parents are licensed to grow azura orchids, so I sort of borrowed it."

Persuaja lifted an eyebrow.

"I know," Zenda said, looking away. "It wasn't really borrowing. But I didn't think anything would go wrong. And then everybody started acting really strange . . ."

Persuaja nodded. "That is the power of the orchid. It affects the auric field of all living beings."

"The auric field?" Zenda asked.

"The energy field that surrounds us all," Persuaja explained. "In humans, the orchid affects emotions, intensifying whatever mood that person is in."

That made sense, Zenda realized. The more time she had been near the orchid, the more impatient she had become.

"I think the orchid gave me a message— a message to stop," Zenda said. "Words popped into my head. That's never happened before."

Persuaja nodded. "I know of your gift, Zenda. The power of the orchid may have intensified that, too."

Zenda nodded. The message from the orchid had certainly felt powerful—and a little bit scary, too.

"The orchid has a much more devastating affect on plants. When its scent makes contact with their auric field, it causes them to grow at a rapid rate," Persuaja continued. "But you probably realized that on your own. Tell me, why were you running with the orchid uncovered like that?"

"Alexandra was going to tell her mother that I had stolen—" Zenda stopped. She had forgotten all about Alex!

"Thanks for everything," she told Persuaja, "but I've got to stop Alex!"

*No Antidote*
*for Stealing*

Zenda ran as fast as she could to the Cobalt School for Girls. To her surprise, she found Alex sitting with her back against the willow tree.

"Alex," Zenda said, catching her breath. "Did you—"

Alexandra shook her head. "No. Once I got here, I didn't feel so angry at you anymore."

"That's because you weren't near the orchid," Zenda said, sitting down next to her. "It definitely made us act the way we did."

Zenda told Alex how she had met Persuaja, and what the psychic had explained about the orchid.

Alex nodded. "I guess that's why it's so dangerous."

"And why the ritual is forbidden," Zenda added. "I guess I can forget about getting my gazing ball back."

The girls sat in silence for a while. Zenda frowned. Things didn't seem finished yet, somehow.

Then she remembered. "Gena and Astrid!" she cried. "Do you think they're okay?"

"We'd better check," Alex said, jumping to her feet.

The girls hurried to Alex's house. They found Persuaja, Gena, and Astrid at the foot of the chestnut tree, ankle deep in chestnuts. Persuaja still held the box containing the orchid.

"Persuaja," Zenda said. "How did you . . . ?" Of course. Persuaja was psychic. It was probably easy for her to find Gena and Astrid.

"Are you two all right?" Alex asked.

"Persuaja gave us the antidote to that orchid," Gena said.

Astrid nodded. "I feel better."

Persuaja gave Alexandra a whiff of the antidote next, just to be safe.

"Perfect!" Alex said, when she was done. "So, nobody has to know about this, right? I didn't tell my mom. Zenda can put the orchid back, and no one will know any better."

*Nobody has to know.* It sounded tempting, but at the same time, the thought gave Zenda a queasy feeling. She looked at Persuaja. The psychic's face didn't reveal any emotion.

"I will make sure Zenda and the orchid get back home safely," Persuaja said. "What happens after that is up to Zenda."

Zenda said good-bye to the girls and she and Persuaja started down the path.

"Sorry I ran off like that," Zenda said. "I guess maybe the orchid hasn't fully worn off yet. It made me really impatient."

Persuaja smiled. "Something tells me you were impatient long before you stole the orchid."

Zenda knew Persuaja was right. "I just wanted to catch up with the other girls," she explained. "After I broke my gazing ball, every-one told me that I would be able to find the pieces on my own. But nobody will tell me how to do it! At this rate, I'll be sixty years old before I get my gazing ball. I can't wait that long!"

"So your parents didn't give you any advice?" Persuaja asked.

"They said the answer was inside me somewhere," Zenda replied.

"And they are right," Persuaja said. They had reached the path to Zenda's house, and Persuaja stopped. "You do have the ability to set things right, on your own."

"But how do you know for sure?" Zenda asked.

Persuaja just smiled in return. *Of course,* Zenda realized. *She is psychic, after all.* That gave her a sudden inspiration.

"How will I do it?" Zenda asked. "You should be able to see what will happen, right?"

Persuaja shook her head. "That is for you to discover," she said. "But if you find you need help, come see me."

She handed Zenda a small lilac card.

*Persuaja—Cosmic Seer*

*The Western Woods*
*inside the Hawthorn Grove*

"Thanks," Zenda said. "I will. And thanks for everything else, too."

Persuaja nodded and handed Zenda the metal box containing the azura orchid. Then she leaned down and whispered into Zenda's ear.

"I can give you one clue about your first musing, Zenda," she said. "You will find it sooner than you think."

Zenda brightened for a moment.

But then Persuaja continued. "But the next musing can't be found in this dimension."

Zenda pondered the words, puzzled. Not in this dimension? What did that mean, exactly? But before she could ask, Persuaja pulled the hood of her cloak over her head, turned, and walked down the path.

Zenda took a deep breath and stared at her house. Lanterns burned in the kitchen, so Verbena and Vetiver must still be awake.

Stealing the orchid had been the wrong thing to do. And there was only one way to make it right.

# A Piece of
# the Future

Zenda walked into the kitchen to find her parents at the kitchen table, drinking tea and talking. They smiled when Zenda walked in.

"How did things go in the greenhouse?" Vetiver asked.

Zenda placed the metal box on the table.

"I have something to tell you," she said.

Zenda took another deep breath and launched into her story. She started from the moment she had decided to sneak into the Lotus Building, and didn't leave anything out.

Her parents looked horrified when she described stealing the orchid. Zenda felt terrible.

"Zenda, I can't stress enough how serious this is," Verbena said. "To play around with an azura orchid . . ."

"I know," Zenda said, avoiding her eyes. "I'm so sorry."

"We should talk to Magenta White immediately," Vetiver said. "I'm not happy with the role Alexandra has played in all of this."

"No!" Zenda cried. "This isn't about Alex. It's about me. I didn't have to do any of those things. Please don't tell her mother. I wouldn't feel right."

Verbena and Vetiver looked at each other. But Verbena shook her head.

"I'm sorry, Zenda," she said. "Stealing an azura orchid has serious consequences for everyone involved. Magenta needs to know."

Zenda felt awful. Alex would never forgive her.

"It may have been Alexandra's idea, but it's really all my fault," Zenda said. "Persuaja was right. The orchid may have made me more impatient, but I was feeling impatient all along. I wanted to find a quick way to solve my problem. But I know better now."

Vetiver tried to smile. "I hope you do, Zenda. I hope you do."

"I'm going to find all of the pieces of my gazing ball on my own," Zenda said. "Even if it takes until I'm sixty!"

At that very moment, a strange tinkling sound filled the air, like the sound of a hundred tiny bells.

The air in front of Zenda shimmered.

Zenda felt her palm tingle and opened her hand. Then she gasped.

In her hand rested a single crystal shard. A faint red mist swirled around it.

"It looks like . . ." Zenda was too excited to finish the words.

"It's a piece of your gazing ball!" Vetiver said, leaning in.

They watched as the red mist separated into tendrils, forming letters. When the mist disappeared, Zenda saw that there were words etched into the glass in red.

*Every flower blooms in its own time.*

"Every flower blooms in its own time." Zenda slowly repeated the words. "It's my first musing!"

Verbena and Vetiver wrapped their arms around Zenda.

"We knew you could do it, starshine," Vetiver whispered.

Verbena left the room. She came back carrying a small wooden box painted with jasmine flowers.

"Delphina gave this to me for my birthday the year your father and I were married," she said. "I think you should have it. You can keep your gazing ball pieces inside it when you find them."

Zenda took the box from her mother. She opened the lid and gingerly placed the crystal shard inside.

"Thanks," Zenda said.

Later that night, Zenda scribbled in her journal under the light of a moonglow flower.

---

*I can't believe I did it! I bound the first piece of my gazing ball. I got my first musing, too.*

At first I didn't understand how it happened. But I think everyone was right when they said the answer was inside me. Once I figured out that being impatient had caused all of my problems, the piece appeared.

I think the musing is about patience, too. 'Every flower blooms in its own time.' When I work in the gardens, I know that every plant has to grow and be fed before it will bloom. I never worry about when it will happen. That's just like me and my gazing ball. I'll find the pieces when the time is right.

Right now, I feel happy and scared at the same time. Persuaja said I would find my next musing in another dimension. I have no idea what that means.

Something tells me I am going to be really surprised when I find out.

Even though I'm scared, it's nice to know that I have people to help me out. Like Camille and Mykal. Persuaja. Even my mother and father.

There's always Luna, too. I know as long as I have her that Delphina will never be far away from me.

I bet if I put my mind to it, I can find the rest of the pieces before I turn thirteen, six months from now. Not that I'm being impatient or anything . . .


Cosmically yours,
Zenda